Pat Hutchins

WHICH WITCH IS WHICH?

Greenwillow Books, New York

Watercolor paints were used for the full-color art.
The text type is ITC Leawood.

Copyright © 1989 by Pat Hutchins

No part of this book may be reproduced without
permission in writing from Greenwillow Books,
105 Madison Ave., New York, N.Y. 10016.
Printed in Singapore by Tien Wah Press
First Edition   10 9 8 7 6 5 4 3 2 1

Library of Congress Cataloging-in-Publication Data
Hutchins, Pat (date)
Which witch is which? / by Pat Hutchins.   p.   cm.
Summary: Although Ella and Emily look alike, their choices
of food, games, and colors at a birthday party help the
reader tell them apart.
ISBN 0-688-06357-8.   ISBN 0-688-06358-6 (lib. bdg.)
[1. Twins—Fiction.   2. Parties—Fiction.   3. Identity—Fiction.
4. Stories in rhyme.]   I. Title.   PZ8.3.H965Wh 1989
[E]—dc19   88-18781   CIP   AC

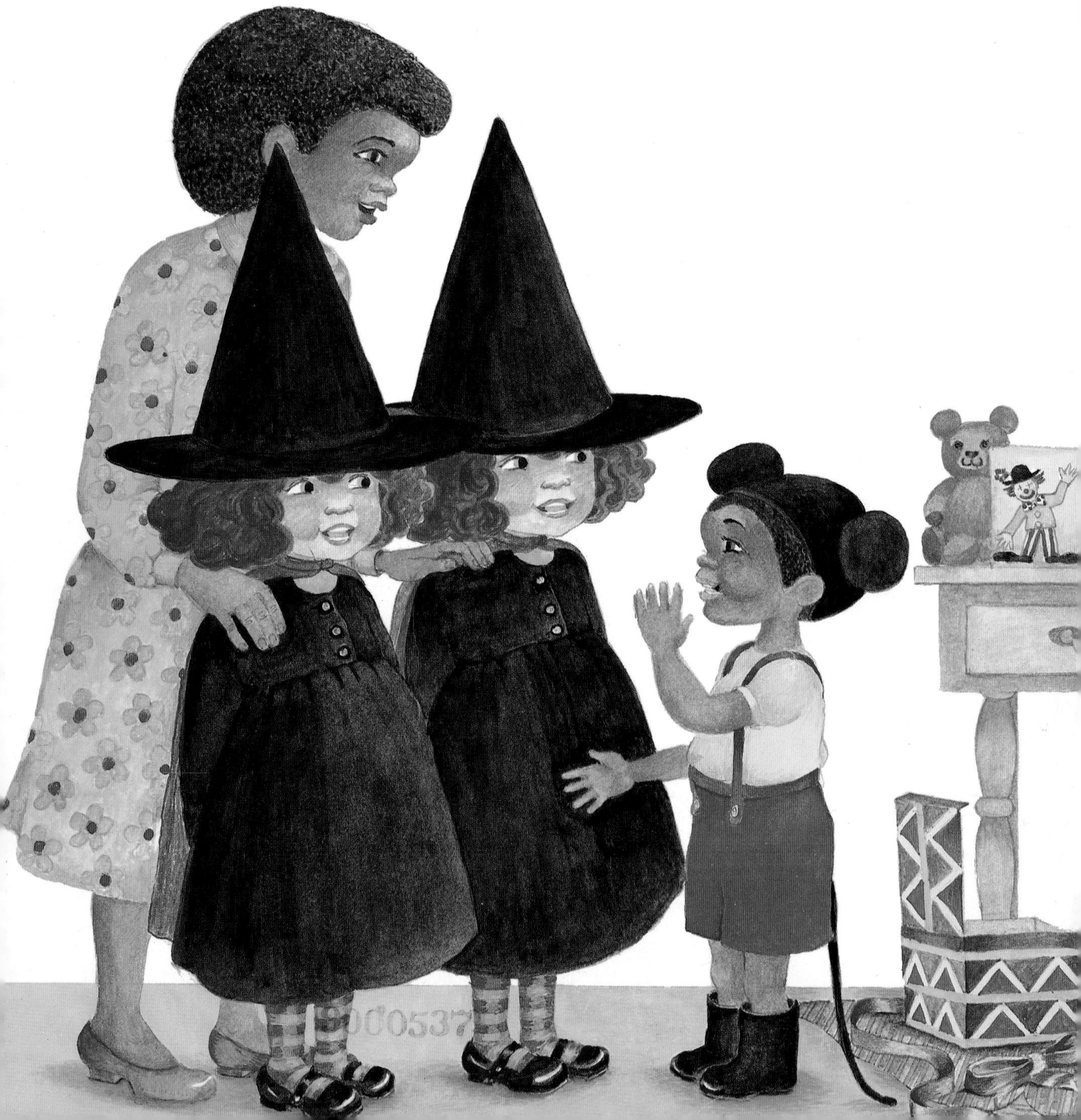

Ella and Emily looked the same,
and were often called
by each other's name.
Ella likes pink, Emily blue.

Which witch is which?

They played tug of war,
three on each side,

and Mouse's mother had to decide
if Ella or Emily's team had won.

Which witch is which?

They all had an ice cream
before the next game.
Cowboy chose strawberry,
Ella the same.

The rest had vanilla
with chocolate chips.

Which witch is which?

They played musical chairs
and skipped and hopped

until one chair was left
and the music stopped.

One witch on the chair,
one witch on the floor.

Which witch is which?

After musical chairs
they had a break,

and Mouse's mother
brought in the cake.
Ella had cake,
Emily did not.

Which witch is which?

At six o'clock
they chose a balloon,
as their parents would be
collecting them soon.

Ella chose pink,
Emily blue.

Which witch is which?